This book is dedicated in loving memory of my Aunt Dora, whose love of picture books forever changed my life. With special thanks to Sarah F. and Sharon C., whose guidance and support helped bring the finch to life. And last but not least, my family—especially Michael, Autumn, and James, who color my world with their patience and love. —A.R.G.

For my parents and my family. And for Pablo, for being by my side in this journey. —H.P.G.

FAMILIUS

Text copyright © 2018 by Annemarie Riley Guertin.
Illustration copyright © 2018 by Helena Pérez García.
All rights reserved.

Published by Familius LLC.
1254 Commerce Way, Sanger, CA 93657.
www.familius.com

Familius books are available at special discounts for bulk purchases, whether for sales promotions or for family or corporate use. For more information, contact Premium Sales at 559-876-2170 or email orders@familius.com. Reproduction of this book in any manner, in whole or in part, without written permission of the publisher is prohibited.

Library of Congress Cataloging-in-Publication Data
2017956665
ISBN 9781945547775
eISBN 9781641700047

Edited by Lindsay Sandberg
Book and jacket design by David Miles

Printed in China

10 9 8 7 6 5 4 3 2 1

First Edition

RETOLD BY

ILLUSTRATIONS BY

ANNEMARIE
RILEY GUERTIN

HELENA
PÉREZ GARCÍA

HOW THE FINCH GOT HIS

COLORS

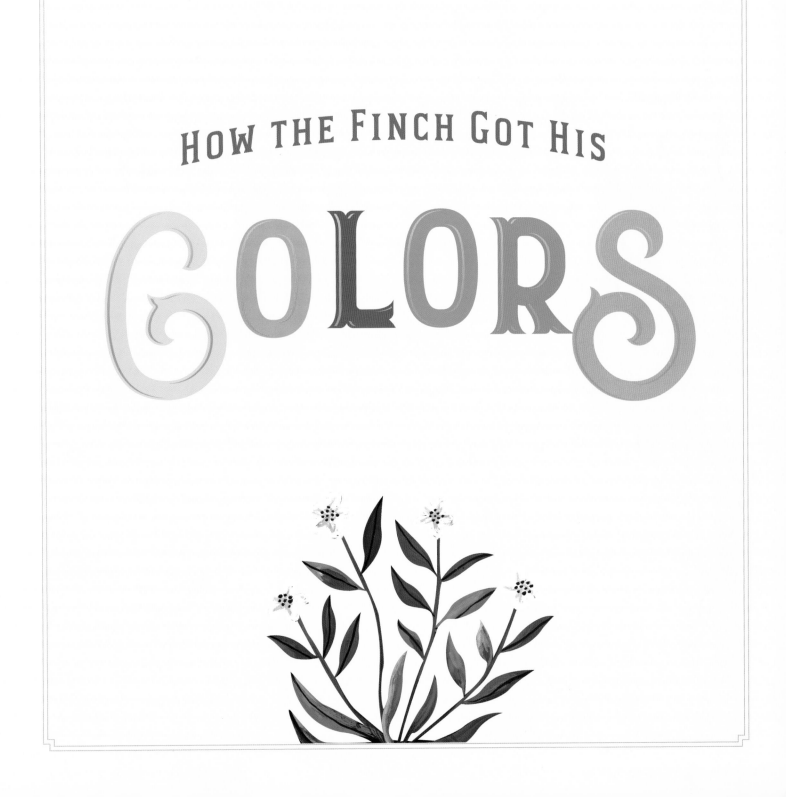

Many years ago, before the world bloomed in magnificent colors, the Earth lay stark and gray. The animals that graced its skies and roamed its lands were the colors of dirt, clay, and stone.

To prepare Earth for its awakening, a great rain fell upon the land. It rained for many days and nights.

On the eleventh day, as if by magic, the rain stopped. As the clouds gave way, the animals looked up to see a rainbow peering down at them.

Awestruck, the animals watched as the bow of light bent toward the Earth. As Rainbow shimmered down, she turned everything in her path into bright, bold colors. The fish in the ocean waters glinted silver, violet, and aquamarine. The yellow duck paddled in the sapphire blue of the pond. And the red fox scurried through the amber forest.

Gazing upon the beauty below him, Great Bird, ruler of the bird kingdom, called out to Rainbow. He was tired of his stone-gray feathers and wished to be a beautiful color. Rainbow agreed, and with one swift kiss, she turned Great Bird from gray to shimmering gold.

The other birds gathered around, and they began to beg and plead
for colors of their own. "Please, Rainbow, we want to be as beautiful
as the other animals! Please give us color too."

Hearing their cries, Rainbow agreed. Great Bird called the birds together and lined them up. The birds chirped and chattered, worried that all of Rainbow's colors would be taken.

Fearing he'd be last, Parrot, the loudest of all the birds, pushed his way to the front of the line. "Green! Make me green!" he called out in his screechy voice.

"Green like the frog that leaps in the pond!"

"I want to be green like the rolling hills below and green like the cactus so spectacular against the barren desert."

And with one swift kiss from Rainbow, Parrot shimmered like an emerald.

One by one, Rainbow gave color to each of the birds. Cardinal, a vibrant red like the fire's flame.

Blue Jay, a shadowy blue like the ocean's hidden depths.

A nd Canary, a brilliant yellow like
the sun's dawning rays.

Rainbow worked hard to please the birds. Soon, the world below her and the skies around her gleamed with the magnificent colors she'd once had. But Rainbow began to grow weary from her hard work. Her colors began to dim until, finally, every last drop of color had been used.

As the birds took flight, Great Bird noticed one small gray bird standing before him. "Come forward, little Gouldian Finch," he said. "Why are you still the color of stone? Do you not wish for a color of your own?" Finch hung his head. "Oh, Great Bird, I waited patiently for my turn, and now all the colors have been chosen. I fear I will be gray forever." Tears began to stream down Finch's cheeks.

Great Bird paused for a moment, thinking about Finch's words. He gazed at the beautiful birds around him and said, "Little Gouldian Finch sat patiently, awaiting his turn. We all shouted and begged to get what we desired. Now there is no color left for him."

The other birds felt sad for their finch friend. They chirped and tweeted until one of them piped up, "How can we right this wrong?"

No sooner had the words been spoken than Rainbow bent down and gathered a splash of color from each of the birds. With one swift kiss, Rainbow worked her magic.

When Finch
opened his
eyes, he looked
down in astonishment.
His once-gray feathers
sparkled brilliantly
with every color of the
rainbow.

And legend has it that from that moment on, the Gouldian finch became known as the most beautiful bird in the world.

Gouldian Finch Fun Facts

- Pronounced \'**güldēən**-\ ("gool-dee-an").
- Native to Northern Australia and New Guinea.
- Lives in grasslands near water.
- Eats seeds.
- Male and female both take turns sitting on the eggs to keep them warm until the babies hatch.
- Baby chicks are born without feathers; they do not become as colorful as their parents until they, too, reach adulthood.
- Rarest type of Gouldian finch has a yellow or golden face.

Discussion Questions

1. What character traits would you say best describe Finch? Great Bird? Parrot?
2. Rainbow shared her colors with the whole world to make it more beautiful. What are some ways *you* could make the world a more beautiful place?
3. What lesson do you think the other birds in this story learned?
4. Why do you think Rainbow gave Finch some of *every* color and not just one? Do you think that was fair? Why or why not?

Bibliography

Miller, Olive Beaupré, ed. "How the Finch Got Her Colors." *The Latch Key of My Bookhouse*. Chicago: The Bookhouse for Children, 1921. https://archive.org/stream/latchkeyofmybook02mill#page/22/mode/2up